Supporting Learning in Schools

To Carey, Alex and Lily

First published 2011 by A & C Black,
an imprint of Bloomsbury Publishing Plc
50 Bedford Square, London WC1B 3DP

www.acblack.com

Copyright © 2011 Dan Tunstall
Illustrations copyright © 2011 Dave Shephard

The rights of Dan Tunstall and Dave Shephard to be identified
as the author and illustrator of this work have been asserted by them
in accordance with the Copyrights, Designs and Patents Act 1988.

ISBN 978-1-4081-5270-6

A CIP catalogue for this book is available from the British Library.

This book is produced using paper that is made from wood
grown in managed, sustainable forests. It is natural, renewable
and recyclable. The logging and manufacturing processes conform
to the environmental regulations of the country of origin.

Printed and bound in Great Britain
by CPI Cox and Wyman, Reading, RG1 8EX

recommended by

www.catchup.org

Catch Up is a not-for-profit charity which
aims to address the problem of
underachievement that has its roots in
literacy and numeracy difficulties.

Contents

Chapter 1

Going off

Me and my mate Tom are heading out of the canteen when Tom nudges me.

"Hey, Andy," he says. "Look who it is."

Coming along the corridor towards us is Tyler Brown. He's new to Weston College.

He started at our school a couple of weeks back, after the Christmas break. He's in Year Ten, same as me. He's walking the way all kids do if they think they're tough. Shoulders back, feet out to the sides.

"Bit of a hard man, I've heard," Tom says.

I laugh.

"Yeah. Right," I say.

Tyler has spotted me. He grins a stupid grin. He knows who I am. Everyone does. I've got a reputation. Andy Cope. Hardest lad in Year Ten. I could sort out most of the Year Elevens and Twelves too. From what I hear, Tyler thinks he can take me on.

"What are you going to do?" Tom asks.

"Dunno," I say. "Let's see what happens."

I look at Tyler Brown. He's got fuzzy red hair and pale skin. About six foot, twelve stone. A big lad. But then, so am I. It's time to find out who the real hard man is.

People around us are moving out of the way. Everyone knows it's about to go off.

Tyler is only a few feet away now. He puts his head down, and for a second I think he's just going to walk past. But then he drops his shoulder and barges into me. I stand my ground and he almost bounces across the corridor.

Tyler blinks and starts to put his hands up, but I'm already all over him. I crack a left hook onto his right ear and down he goes. Works every time. Anyone I hit is going over.

Tyler pushes himself onto his hands and knees. There's pain and fear in his eyes, but it looks like he might be ready to have another go. I'm about to swing a kick into his side when an arm tightens round my neck and yanks me backwards.

In one move I duck down, break out of the hold, spin on the spot and get ready to lamp someone else. But then I stop. It's not another lad. It's Mr Gibbs, the PE teacher.

For someone who teaches sport, Gibbo isn't the most healthy-looking. His face is fat and red and puffy. He always looks like he's been holding his breath for about five minutes.

"Andy Cope, Tyler Brown," he shouts, eyeballs popping. "Mr Maxwell's office, now!"

Chapter 2

Mum on my case

I've been sitting outside Mr Maxwell's office for half an hour. Tyler Brown has already been in. His dad turned up ten minutes after getting a phone call from the school.

When he came out, Tyler gave me that stupid grin again. Looks like he's been let off. Bet I won't be. I puff out a deep breath and stare at the floor.

Five minutes later my mum arrives. She looks angry and worn out. She dumps her bag on a chair and sits next to me.

I open my mouth to speak. Mum holds her hand up.

"Don't even bother," she says. "Mr Maxwell has told me all I need to know."

My guts twist.

"Mum…" I say.

Mum isn't listening.

"You're going to get me sacked," she says. "This is the third time this term I've had to tell my boss you've been taken ill at school. I couldn't bear to tell her the truth."

This isn't fair.

"But Mum, this Tyler kid started it." My voice goes up as I try to make my point. "I had to do something."

"And all you could think of was punching him?"

"Mum," I say. "You can't let people get away with stuff. This isn't a nursery. It's all about survival round here."

Mum takes her coat off and puts it across her knees.

"Can't you ever just let it go?" she says.

I squeeze my fists. I'm angry she doesn't understand.

"You don't get it, do you?" I say. "I've got a reputation to keep up."

"Don't be so silly," Mum says.

There's nothing silly about my reputation. To be top lad in Year Ten means something. It makes me somebody. I'm not good at many things. I feel stupid in most of my classes. Fighting is the only thing I've got to be proud of. And it gives me a buzz.

Mum starts up again.

"You're just like your dad. He always wanted to settle things with his fists."

"Well, you married him," I say. I didn't mean to say that, but it comes out before I can think.

Now there's a hurt look in Mum's eyes. I'm about to say sorry when the office door swings open.

"Ah, Mrs Cope," Mr Maxwell says. "I'm glad you could make it. Hope I haven't dragged you away from anything important?"

"No, Mr Maxwell," Mum lies. "Nothing important."

Chapter 3

Mr Maxwell on my case

Inside the office, me and Mum sit in front
of the desk. Mr Maxwell sits on the other
side. I look around the room. Nothing has
changed since the last time I was in here. The
shelves are covered in the same clay pots.

There's the same fruit bowl full of wooden apples and pears. I'm not sure why he has stupid wooden fruit in his room.

Mr Maxwell puts his elbows on the desk and folds his fingers together. He's bald with a thin ring of hair round the back and sides of his head. He reminds me of a vulture.

"Andrew," he says, voice stern. "You are starting to cause me a lot of bother."

There's nothing much I can say. I'm waiting to hear what he's going to do to me. Give me a detention? Suspend me?

Mr Maxwell clears his throat.

"However, I've agreed with Mr Brown that Tyler should just be given a warning.

So it's only fair that I say the same to you. This time, there will be no more action taken."

I stare down at my shoes.

"Andy!" Mum says, poking me. "Mr Maxwell says he won't take action this time."

I nod. If Mum thinks I'm going to act pleased, she's wrong. The silence goes on and on.

Mr Maxwell lines up some pencils.

"You know, Andrew," he says, "sooner or later I'll run out of things I can do with you. You've been suspended before. It may be that I have to exclude you."

I yawn. I know it's true. But I don't really care.

Mr Maxwell rubs his hand across his bald head.

"What you need is a way to channel your energy. Are there any sports you like?"

I laugh. Gibbo banned me from the football team for fighting in PE. I nearly chinned him half an hour ago. He's not going to change his mind any time soon.

Mr Maxwell carries on.

"You're a big lad. Have you ever thought about boxing?"

"Dunno. Not really," I mutter.

Mr Maxwell looks at my mum.

"How would you feel about Andrew boxing, Mrs Cope?"

"I'd support anything that kept him out of trouble, Mr Maxwell," she says.

Mr Maxwell turns back towards me.

"Do you like boxing, Andrew?"

"Nah. Boxing's for wusses," I sneer.

Mum claps a hand across her mouth. "Andy!" she hisses.

"Sorry," I say.

"Well," Mr Maxwell says, "perhaps you should give it a try. Keep an open mind. There's a gym in town, the Blue Corner Boxing Club."

"It's at some pub, isn't it?" I say.

"That's right. It's right in the centre of Langton. Above the King's Head on Church Lane. It's run by a man called Terry Reed. An ex-pro boxer. So do you think you might see what it's like?" Mr Maxwell asks.

Mum looks at me like she's hoping I'll say yes.

"It's Saturday tomorrow," she says. "You could pop down in the morning."

"Maybe," I say.

Chapter 4

Becky on my case

Ten minutes later, I'm back in class. The afternoon drags on. At 3.20 the bell rings. I leave the ICT room and head for the exit.

Becky is waiting for me in the same place as always. Sitting on the low wall round the flowerbeds at the front of the school. We've been going out for more than two years. She's got her back to me, but I know it's her. I can see her blonde hair tied back and the flower-print bag over the shoulder of her green coat.

As I walk towards her, she turns round. Straight away, I see I'm in trouble. Her face is twisted into a frown. There's a stern look in her blue eyes.

"What's up?" I ask.

"I know about what happened with Tyler Brown," she says.

My heart sinks. News travels fast at Weston College.

"Oh, that," I say, smiling. "It was no big deal."

"That's not what I heard," Becky says. "Is Mr Maxwell going to suspend you again?"

"Nah," I say. "Not this time."

I try another smile.

Becky shakes her head. She stands up and starts to walk towards the gates.

"Hey, come on," I say, catching up with her. "Tyler Brown started it. He was acting hard."

"There's always a reason why you have to thump someone, isn't there?" Becky says.

I can't find anything to say.

"You've changed in the last year," she goes on. "Tom's the only mate you've got left. You've scared everyone else off. Why do you have to be like this?"

I think about telling her the truth. About what my reputation means to me. About how hitting people is the only thing I'm any good at. But I don't think she'd listen.

We walk in silence. Out of the gates and along the edge of the playing fields. It's cold and our breath is coming out in blasts of white.

I try to get things back on track.

"Mum and Mr Maxwell think I should take up boxing," I say.

"Really?" Becky says.

"Yeah. There's a gym in town. The Blue Corner Boxing Club. Some old ex-fighter runs it."

We're at the turning into Becky's road now.

"Are you going to check it out?" she asks.

"You think I should?" I say.

Becky nods.

"I think you should do something," she says. "Anything. At the moment you're going nowhere."

My stomach turns over. Becky is still angry with me.

"Yeah." My words dry up after that.

"Honestly?" Becky says. "You need to sort your life out. Because if you don't, we're finished. It's not nice going out with a thug."

I'm shocked. I reach out to touch her, but she pulls away and steps up to her front door.

"See you, Andy," she says.

Chapter 5

Decision

It's grim at home tonight. Mum doesn't want to talk. She's still really narked about this afternoon. We eat our dinner in silence, then I clear the table.

"Right then," I say. "I'm going out."

Mum laughs.

"No, you're not," she says. "You're grounded."

"What about the boxing club? I thought you wanted me to go tomorrow," I say.

"That's different," Mum says.

"Are you going to tell my dad about what happened today?" I ask.

Mum pulls a face. She's only thirty-seven, but tonight she looks much older.

"What's the point?" she says.

I know what she means. We hardly ever see my dad. It's been three years since he left. When he does come round, he's always drunk.

Over Mum's shoulder, I catch sight of a photo of my dad and me. It was taken when I was about ten. My hair was quite blond back then. It was quite long too.

Up in my room I stand in front of the mirror, looking at myself. I'm fifteen now and I've changed a bit. My hair isn't blond any more. It's brown and cut very short. My face is long and thin, not chubby like it used to be. But some things are still the same. The eyes. The nose. And if I squint my eyes, it's still that kid in the photo staring back at me.

I flop onto my bed. I sometimes wish I could be ten again. Life seemed a lot easier back then. Everyone has been on my case today. Tyler Brown. Mr Maxwell. Becky. Mum.

It's doing my head in. I feel like punching something. But it won't do me any good.

Five minutes of staring at the walls and I'm getting bored. I put the TV on, but all five channels are showing rubbish. I don't get Sky up here. I text Becky, but she doesn't reply.

I grab my laptop and go online. I check my emails and my Facebook page. Nothing. The night is going nowhere.

But then an idea pops into my head. The boxing club. I wonder if it has a website?

I type *blue corner boxing club* into the Google box. Right away, I see I need to narrow down my search. There are hundreds of Blue Corner Boxing Clubs.

I try again. This time I put *blue corner boxing club langton*. Bingo. One more click and I'm there.

It's pretty basic. The screen shows a few clip-art pictures of boxing gloves and punch-bags. There is a list of opening times and the prices. *£2.00 a session, £1.50 for members*. There's an address and a contact number. That's it.

I shake my head and go back to the Google home page.

Mr Maxwell said the club was run by a bloke called Terry Reed. I Google his name: *terry reed boxer*. He's easy to find. His full boxing record is on BoxStats.com.

Terry Reed

Birth date: 13/05/1955
Division: Middleweight
Active: 1975-1992
Title(s): Midlands Area
Champion
Height: 5'9"
Country: United Kingdom
Address: Langton UK
Born: Langton UK
Fights: 84
Won: 39 (KO 21)
Lost: 41 (KO 0)
Drew: 4
Rounds boxed: 528
KO%: 25

I laugh. Terry Reed lost more fights than he won. It's true that he never got knocked out. But he never went higher than local title level either.

I look at his photo. He's in his boxing gear. It was probably taken back in the 80s. He's got skinny little legs but his chest and arms are huge. His hair is dark, brushed forwards. His eyebrows are thick with scars. His nose is totally flat.

I switch the laptop off and close it. Lying back on my bed, I think about tomorrow.

Should I give the Blue Corner a try? The way Terry Reed looks, he can't have got out of the way of a punch in his whole career.

I doubt there's much he could tell me about fighting.

Going to the boxing club might be a waste of time. But it also might get Mum and Mr Maxwell and Becky off my back.

Two more minutes and I've made my mind up. I'll give it a go.

Chapter 6

The Blue Corner

It's a twenty-minute walk from my house to the middle of Langton. Although it's a Saturday morning, everything is quiet. The pavements are crunchy with frost.

The King's Head is about a hundred metres up Church Lane.

Round the back of the pub, a set of steps leads to a brown wooden door. On the wall above is a faded sign:

The Blue Corner Boxing Club

I go up the stairs and push the door open.

The first thing I notice is how warm it is in the gym. It's dark, and the place looks like it hasn't been cleaned for years. It doesn't smell too good.

The walls are lined with tatty old fight posters. Blue and red mats are dotted about the dusty wooden floor. In the centre, with three steps going up to it, is the boxing ring.

The place is mega-busy. There are lads and girls. All ages, all races. Asian kids. Black kids. White kids. Chinese kids. Everywhere I look, someone is stretching or sparring or shadow-boxing or bench-pressing.

There's a shower area over to the right, and in the left-hand corner is what looks like an office. There's a bloke standing in the doorway. Terry Reed. His hair is greyer now, but apart from that, he hasn't changed since the photo on BoxStats.com was taken. He's probably not even a pound over his fighting weight. He's wearing a black sleeveless T-shirt. His arms still look like they're carved out of stone.

I pull my bag onto my shoulder and head across.

"Morning, lad," Terry says, his voice a low growl. "First time, is it?"

I nod. I fish in my pocket and pull out two pound coins.

"That's right," I say. "I'm Andy. Andy Cope. Two quid a session, yeah?"

Terry holds up his hand. I notice some of his knuckles are lumpy and swollen.

"First time is free," he says. "You got some kit to wear?"

I hold up my sports bag.

"Right. Good," Terry says. "Well, get yourself sorted and you can make a start with your warm-up."

"Okay," I say.

Terry goes into the office while I strip down to my sports gear. I stuff my street clothes back into my bag, stick my trainers on and stand up. I'm ready for action.

Terry talked about doing a warm-up. That doesn't sound like much fun. I haven't come to a boxing gym to roll around on a mat. I've come here to punch things.

Up on the wall, boxing gloves hang together in pairs. I'm not a big boxing fan, but I know there are different types of gloves. There are sparring gloves and speed bag gloves. What I'm looking for is a pair of punch-bag gloves.

And there they are. Blue leather with white Velcro straps. I grab a pair and pull them on. Then I go off to thump one of those heavy bags.

Chapter 7

Fight!

I've been pounding away at a punch-bag for a while when I see Terry coming my way. He watches me for a few seconds. Then he shakes his head.

I'm out of breath, so I stop punching.

"What's up?" I ask.

"You're puffing a bit," Terry says. "You've got to pace yourself."

I shrug and throw a few more punches at the bag.

Terry carries on looking at me.

"You need to think about how you're standing," he says. "The way you are now, feet together, you won't get any power in your punches."

I laugh. He wouldn't be saying that if he'd seen me at Weston College yesterday. I pull a face. Slowly, very slowly, I move one foot forwards.

Terry's still looking at me.

"You're right-handed, are you?" he asks.

"Mmm," I say.

"So don't just swing away like a madman. Lead with your left hand. Use your right hand to guard your chin, then bring it over the top."

I do as he says. Couple of lefts, then a big right. I follow it up with a volley of left and right hooks.

Terry puts his hands on his head.

"No. Jab. Jab-jab-jab-jab-jab. It's the boxer's most important punch. And get your guard up."

I stop what I'm doing and spread my arms out wide. I'm already sick of this. I don't need some old geezer telling me how to fight.

A bloke who lost forty-one times. I know what I'm doing. In fact, I'm an expert.

"Look, mate," I say. "The bag isn't going to hit me back."

Terry nods. There's a little smile on his face.

"No. You're right. You know what you're doing. Maybe this would be a good time for you to have a go at sparring."

"Now you're talking," I say.

Two minutes later I'm sitting on a stool in the corner of the ring. My knuckles have been wrapped and I've changed out of the punch-bag gloves and into a pair made for sparring.

I've got a big padded head-guard on and a rubber gum-shield. I just need to find out who I'm fighting.

There's someone coming up the steps into the other corner. He's wearing the same sort of head-guard as me, but I can see who it is. I almost feel like laughing out loud.

It's Jack Mills from school. He's in my year. He's just a skinny little kid. He's probably nine stone, at the most.

Terry parts the ropes and steps into the ring. He's going to be the ref.

"Okay lads," he says. "Keep it clean. No rough stuff. Let's see what you've got."

I slam my gloves together. This is going to be fantastic. Giving someone a thump and no danger of getting into trouble. I'm getting that buzz I always get when it's all kicking off.

Terry backs out of the way and I step forward, throwing hard shots with both hands.

Thirty seconds in, I've not landed a punch. Jack has hit me with a few jabs, but that's about it. I keep moving forward, looking to land a punch on Jack.

I start to throw a right, but that's when Jack catches me. It's a sneaky left hand, smashing into my side, under my elbow.

In a split second, all the wind is knocked out of my lungs. Pain is spreading through my ribs and filling my whole body. I slide down against the ropes.

Terry stands over me.

"Time out," he says.

Chapter 8

Knock-out

Back in the corner, I sit on my stool, sucking in air. I check to see if anyone else in the gym saw what just happened. Doesn't look like it. Everyone is busy getting on with their own thing.

Terry looks across.

"Slipped," I say. "It's these trainers."

Terry's heard that story before.

"Right," he says, smiling. "You ready to go again?"

I nod, and Terry says, "Okay. Time in."

I push myself up off the stool and stare across the ring. Jack's bouncing up and down, making his way towards me. There's a grim look on his face. I start grinning. This time, there will be no mistakes. I'm bigger than Jack. I'm stronger than he is. I'm harder. Anyone I hit, they're going over.

I take a deep breath and bite down on my gum-shield. Ducking to my right, I swing a huge hook. It's on target, but Jack gets his left glove up and blocks the punch.

I throw another right. This time Jack moves his head half an inch and the punch misses him.

No matter what I do, I can't land a proper punch on Jack. It's like chucking darts at a fly. Every time I think I've got him, he skips out of range. He's only little, but the way he moves, I'd say he's been boxing for years.

The pain in my ribs is coming back. Punching thin air is tiring. It's getting harder to breathe. I'm puffing like an old steam engine. I've blown myself out.

And Jack knows it. Suddenly, instead of keeping out of the way, he's coming forward, bobbing and weaving, throwing punches of his own.

It's like being caught in a hail of gunfire. The punches seem to be coming from everywhere. And wherever I put my gloves, Jack keeps finding the holes in my guard. Two lefts crash into the side of my head. Jabs are drilling into my face.

I duck down, but an upper-cut hits me on the nose. I feel sick and dizzy and I can taste blood in my mouth. This shouldn't be happening. I try to grab and hold, but Jack's too fast. He swings a right cross. I see it coming, but it's too late.

The next thing I know, Terry Reed is bending over me. His face is a blur at first, but then it comes into focus.

"You okay, Andy?" he asks.

I spit my gum-shield out and push myself up on my elbows. My cheeks are burning red. Partly it's because of Jack's punches. Mainly it's shame.

"Stay down until your head clears," Terry says.

I ignore him. My brain is still spinning, but I'm up onto my feet now. Jack is coming across. He looks like he's going to say sorry. I don't want to hear it.

Before he can reach me, I duck between the ropes. I pull off my gloves, hand-wraps and head-guard. I grab my sports bag and I head for the exit.

Chapter 9

Back to school

The ringing of my alarm clock wakes me up. I roll over and switch it off. And then it hits me. It's Monday. I've got to go to school. But I don't know if I can. Everyone there is going to know about the Blue Corner, and what happened between Jack and me.

My reputation is going to be ruined.

I don't speak a word while I wash, put my school gear on, eat breakfast and get ready to leave the house. As I'm going out of the front door, Mum stops me.

"Andy, is there something wrong?" She's worried about me. "You've been really quiet all weekend."

"No, Mum," I say. "Everything is fine."

Mum looks right into my eyes. She can see I'm lying. But before she can ask anything else, I'm on the street.

It's cold and grey this morning. The frost has gone, but there's an icy wind blowing. I walk fast and keep my head down all the way to Weston College. I don't call for Becky.

English is the first lesson. It's as boring as ever. Miss Brady hands out some worksheets, then sits at her desk tapping at a laptop.

I don't bother to write anything. I just stare at my table. Every now and then, I check out what's going on around me. I think I will see people looking at me and laughing. But no-one is.

It's the same story in my next lesson. I look for people talking about me, laughing, taking the mick. Saying that I'm not the daddy any more. But again – nothing. It doesn't make sense. You can't keep anything quiet at Weston College.

As I'm passing the library at break time, Becky steps out in front of me.

"Hello, stranger," she says.

I try to smile. My bottom lip is a bit swollen. I hope Becky doesn't see it.

"How was the boxing gym?" she asks.

I look into Becky's eyes. She must have heard about what happened. But if she's acting, she's very good at it.

"It was okay," I say. I don't think I'm as good at acting as Becky is.

"Cool," she says, and she gives me a kiss. "Anyway, got to dash. Catch you later."

In the tutor room, Tom is waiting for me. It's the first time I've seen him today.

"Alright, Andy?" he says.

"Yeah," I say.

Tom looks at me.

"What's up, mate?" he asks.

"You really don't know? You've not heard people saying things?" I say.

Tom shakes his head. But he can see that I don't believe him.

"It's true," he says. "I've not heard anything. Why? What should I have heard?"

"Nothing," I say.

I've got to know what's going on. And there's only one way I can do that.

I need to talk to Jack Mills.

Chapter 10

Boxing, not fighting

Jack Mills is hard to find. I've tried the canteen. I've tried the music block. I've tried the ICT room. I'm running out of places to look, and break time will be over in five minutes.

Finally, I walk down to the sports hall. There's a game of six-a-side going on and Jack is watching. As I head towards him, one of his mates sees me coming. He nudges Jack.

"Jack," I say. "I want a word."

Jack looks a bit on-edge.

"Yeah, okay," he says. "What's up?"

"Can we go outside to do this?" I ask.

Jack leaves his bag with his mates and follows me out of a fire exit. We walk outside and sit on a bench. It seems to be even colder than it was on the way to school. The sky is dark grey and the wind is blowing stronger and stronger.

I don't mess around.

"So what's the story?" I ask.

"What do you mean?" Jack says.

"How come you've not told everyone what happened on Saturday?" I ask him.

Jack looks surprised.

"Why would I?" he asks.

"Because you beat the crap out of me," I say. "If you can fight like that, you're one of the hardest kids around. I mean, really, you're top lad in Year Ten."

Jack is shaking his head.

"On Saturday, that wasn't fighting," he says. "That was boxing. There's a big difference. Boxing isn't about being hard. It's about using your brain, using your skills."

I nod slowly. I get it now. It's like a bulb coming on in my head. I suddenly feel pretty stupid.

"Right. So you wouldn't go around talking about Saturday?"

"No way," Jack says. "Always respect your opponent. And what happens in the Blue Corner stays in the Blue Corner."

"Right," I say again. "It's funny, though. Until Saturday, I thought boxing was for wusses. Turns out I was the wuss. Think I'll steer clear of the Blue Corner in future."

Jack shrugs.

"It's up to you," he says. "But it was only your first time. You had some good moves. You've got good power in your punches."

"You reckon?" I ask.

"Yeah," he says. "I'm good at rolling with the punches, but a couple of those right-handers of yours… I was seeing stars for a second or two."

I look at my right fist. I nod and smile. I feel a whole lot better. Jack talked about respect. He's got my respect now. And for him to have good words to say about my boxing, well, that means something.

Jack carries on.

"If I was you, I'd have another crack at it. If you start coming a few times a week, listen to what Terry has to say, you could make a decent boxer."

"So does Terry know his stuff?" I ask. "I mean, he lost about forty fights, didn't he?"

"Yeah," Jack says. "But you need to look at who he went in with. Alan Minter. Tony Sibson. Nigel Benn. He got beat a lot of times, but he gave everyone a hard night. Even the top, top fighters."

I feel bad about laughing at Terry's boxing record now. I'm no boxing nut, but I've heard of those names. Some of them were world champions.

"So what do you reckon, then?" Jack asks. "You going to give Blue Corner another go?"

I turn it over in my head.

"You know what?" I say. "I think I might."

Chapter 11

Seconds out

That was January. Today, it's April. A lot has changed.

I can't believe I thought about giving up on boxing. It's become a big, big part of my life. I'm at the Blue Corner five or six times a week. And that's not all that's different.

It's amazing, but I've not been in trouble at school since that Friday afternoon in Mr Maxwell's office. Not once.

Even Tyler Brown and I are okay with each other. We're not mates exactly, and he still has a stupid walk. But we grin and nod if we pass each other in the corridor.

I don't really know what made me change. I suppose it was lots of things. When Becky said she'd break up with me if I didn't stop the fighting. Then what happened the first time I went to the gym. Being hard started to look a bit stupid. And I think maybe I just got fed up with people being fed up with me.

Whatever. I don't feel like I need to go around punching people any more. I'm not interested in my reputation. Being hard is kids' stuff. I do all my punching at the Blue Corner.

And that's where I am now. It's a Friday night, and I'm sitting in Terry's office. I'm wearing a blue vest and matching satin shorts. And I'm getting gloved up for my first proper contest.

The Blue Corner is taking on the King Street Club from Skipley, a couple of miles down the road. I'm paired against a lad called Steve Jones. Three two-minute rounds. Our match is on next.

Outside in the hall, I hear the final bell
for the contest before mine. There's clapping
and cheering as the MC reads out the scores,
and then the Blue Corner fighter is on his way
back to the office.

It's Jack Mills.

"I won," he says, grinning.

"Nice one," I say.

Terry appears in the doorway.

"Okay, Andy. Time to go."

I nod and bang my red gloves together. As
I stand up and head for the door, my stomach
turns over. But it's no big deal. I've been
looking forward to this.

The clapping starts again as I walk out into the gym. The floor is covered with chairs we've borrowed from the pub downstairs. Every seat is taken. The room is dark, but bright white lights are shining above the ring.

Going up the three wooden steps, I duck between the ropes. Terry climbs up behind me. Steve Jones is already in the other corner. He's a bit shorter than me. Big shoulders, thick neck. Should be a good test.

I look into the crowd. A couple of rows back, I see Tom. Mum's sitting next to him, and Becky's in the next seat along. Dad's not here, but he texted earlier on, wishing me luck.

Mum and Becky smile and wave. They're proud of me. And it feels great.

The MC is a fat bloke in a tight-fitting dinner jacket. He's starting to read out the details of our fight. I'm not really listening. I'm right in the zone, ready to go. Seconds later, the MC is climbing out through the ropes. The referee, a tough-looking black geezer with a shaved head, is calling us to the middle of the ring. I stare into Steve Jones's eyes. He's not scared. But then, neither am I.

We touch gloves and I take a couple of steps back. I shake my arms and roll my head left and right. I test the grip of my new boxing boots on the canvas.

Terry checks that my head-guard is on tightly and slips my gum-shield into my mouth.

"Remember what I said," he whispers. "Jab-jab-jab-jab-jab."

I nod. Jab. Move. Keep my guard up. Think about footwork. Pace myself. I do what Terry says now. He's the expert, not me.

I look down at the time-keeper. He's ready to ring the first bell.

"Seconds out… Round one."